D0549000

man

Phonics Friends

Marcus and the Mail
The Sound of M

mail

The
**Child's
World**

By Joanne Meier and Cecilia Minden

moon

The Child's World

Published in the United States of America
by The Child's World®
PO Box 326
Chanhassen, MN 55317-0326
800-599-READ
www.childsworld.com

A special thank you to the Melaniphy family.
Conor, you were great!

The Child's World®: Mary Berendes, Publishing Director

Editorial Directions, Inc.: E. Russell Primm, Editorial
Director and Project Editor; Katie Marsico, Associate
Editor; Judith Shiffer, Associate Editor and School Media
Specialist; Linda S. Koutris, Photo Researcher and
Selector

The Design Lab: Kathleen Petelinsek, Design and Page
Production

Photographs ©: Photo setting and photography by Romie
and Alice Flanagan/Flanagan Publishing Services: cover,
4, 6, 8, 10, 12, 14, 16; Getty Images/Stone: 18; Corbis/
NASA: 20.

Library of Congress Cataloging-in-Publication Data
Meier, Joanne.
  Marcus and the mail : the sound of M / by Joanne
Meier and Cecilia Minden.
    p. cm. — (Phonics friends)
  Summary: Simple text featuring the sound of the letter
"m" tells about Marcus receiving something in the mail.
  ISBN 1-59296-300-5 (library bound : alk. paper) [1.
English language—Phonetics. 2. Reading.] I. Meier,
Joanne D. II. Title. III. Series.
  PZ7.M6539Mar 2004
  [E]—dc22   2004003535

Note to parents and educators:

The Child's World® has created Phonics Friends with the goal of exposing children to engaging stories and pictures that assist in phonics development. The books in the series will help children learn the relationships between the letters of written language and the individual sounds of spoken language. This contact helps children learn to use these relationships to read and write words.

The books in this series follow a similar format. An introductory page, to be read by an adult, introduces the child to the phonics feature, or sound, that will be highlighted in the book. Read this page to the child, stressing the phonic feature. Help the student learn how to form the sound with her mouth. The Phonics Friends story and engaging photographs follow the introduction. At the end of the story, word lists categorize the feature words into their phonic element. Additional information on using these lists is on The Child's World® Web site listed at the top of this page.

Each book in this series has been carefully written to meet specific readability requirements. Close attention has been paid to elements such as word count, sentence length, and vocabulary. Readability formulas measure the ease with which the text can be read and understood. Each Phonics Friends book has been analyzed using the Spache readability formula. For more information on this formula, as well as the levels for each of the books in this series please visit The Child's World® Web site.

Reading research suggests that systematic phonics instruction can greatly improve students' word recognition, spelling, and comprehension skills. The Phonics Friends series assists in the teaching of phonics by providing students with important opportunities to apply their knowledge of phonics as they read words, sentences, and text.

This is the letter *m*.

In this book, you will read words that have the *m* sound as in:

mail, milk, mother, and *man.*

Today is a big day for Marcus.

He might get some mail.

Marcus makes his bed.

He puts most of his toys away.

Marcus makes his breakfast.

He likes toast and milk.

After breakfast, Marcus gets dressed. He can do most of it by himself. His mother helps with the rest.

Marcus and his mother get the mail. Most of it is for Marcus's mother.

Some mail is for Marcus!

It is a new book.

That makes Marcus happy.

"May I read it now?" asks Marcus.

"Yes, you may," says Mother.

"Let's read it together."

Marcus and his mother read the book. It is about a man who walked on the moon.

"One day I will walk on the moon," says Marcus. Would you like to walk on the moon like Marcus?

Fun Facts

Do you think you might want to visit the moon? You'll probably find it very different from life on earth. There is no water on the surface of the moon, and there aren't any clouds. Instead of earthquakes, the moon has what are called "moonquakes." Also, time passes more slowly on the moon than it does on earth. One day on the moon is 655 hours long!

Suppose you live in Missouri and need to mail a letter to a friend in California. You know that your friend will receive his letter in the mail about two to three days after you send it. In the 1800s, however, it would probably have taken about 10 days for the letter to reach your friend. Employees of a mail service called the Pony Express rode on horseback between Missouri and California and delivered letters and packages along the way.

Activity

Studying the Moon

On a clear night, you can see the moon in the sky. If you want a closer view, ask your parents if they have a telescope. A telescope is a device that makes faraway objects appear to be closer. With the help of a telescope, you will be able to see the surface of the moon more clearly. You might also be able to see several stars and possibly even some planets!

To Learn More

Books
About the Sound of M
Ballard, Peg, and Cynthia Klingel. *Malls: The Sound of M*. Chanhassen, Minn.: The Child's World, 2000.

About Mail
Kottke, Jan. *A Day with a Mail Carrier*. Danbury, Conn.: Children's Press, 2000.
Tunnell, Michael O., and Ted Rand (illustrator). *Mailing May*. New York: Greenwillow Books, 1997.

About the Moon
Banks, Kate, and Georg Hallensleber (illustrator). *And if the Moon Could Talk*. New York: Frances Foster Books, 1998.
Gibbons, Gail. *The Moon Book*. New York: Holiday House, 1997.

About Mothers
Horlacher, Bill, Kathy Horlacher, and Kathryn Hutton (illustrator). *I'm Glad I'm Your Mother*. Cincinnati: Standard Publishing, 1996.
Lasky, Kathryn, and LeUyen Pham (illustrator). *Before I Was Your Mother*. San Diego: Harcourt, 2003.

Web Sites
Visit our home page for lots of links about the Sound of M:
http://www.childsworld.com/links.html

Note to Parents, Teachers, and Librarians: We routinely check our Web links to make sure they're safe, active sites—so encourage your readers to check them out!

M Feature Words

Proper Names
Marcus

Feature Words in Initial Position
made

mail

make

man

may

might

milk

moon

most

mother

Feature Word in Medial Position
himself

About the Authors

Joanne Meier, PhD, has worked as an elementary school teacher and university professor. She earned her BA in early childhood education from the University of South Carolina, and her MEd and PhD in education from the University of Virginia. She currently works as a literacy consultant for schools and private organizations. Joanne Meier lives with her husband Eric, and spends most of her time chasing her two daughters, Kella and Erin, and her two cats, Sam and Gilly, in Charlottesville, Virginia.

Cecilia Minden, PhD, directs the Language and Literacy Program at the Harvard Graduate School of Education. She is a reading specialist with classroom and administrative experience in grades K–12. She earned her PhD in reading education from the University of Virginia. Cecilia and her husband Dave Cupp enjoy sharing their love of reading with their granddaughter Chelsea.